Cici and Molly

The Secret Den

ISBN-13: 978-1478171430
ISBN-10: 147817143X

Cici and Molly

The Secret Den

by Kasia Brown

Illustrated by Nanuli Burduli

For Marie-Louise, Ruby and Willa. Our friendship reminds me of Cici and Molly and how kind you are to me as friends.

Contents

Prologue

On a cold stormy night, in a poor part of town, there was a lone scream. It was a mother giving birth to twin girls. Although she was upset, she did not let her face show it.

She was upset because she could not afford to have two children. She looked at both of them. Which one should she give away?

Chapter One

At Cici's mansion it was her 8th birthday! This year, she got 36 presents.

"But last year I got 36 presents as well," complained Cici.

"Yes, darling," said her step-mother, "but this year they are bigger presents."

"I don't care if they're bigger," said

Cici. "I just want more!"

For her party, Cici invited all her friends (well, everyone she knew even if you wouldn't really call them friends). The party was at the cinema. Cici took her cat, Sally, and her tortoise, Slodge, to the cinema with her. Soon, she got bored of the film so

she started dressing up her pets. They didn't like it so they decided to run away –

Slodge was on Sally's back.

Chapter Two

On the same day, it was Molly's birthday. Molly didn't celebrate birthdays as much  as Cici. She only got one present from her Mum. It was a daisy chain which her mum had picked from the churchyard and she received no presents from anyone else.

Molly's brothers did not really like her.

Their four Labrador dogs – Chester, Jack, Bonnie and Bisou - were her only friends.

She didn't go out celebrating. She just stayed at home and had a party with her family.

There wasn't a large birthday cake, rather her family only had one scone to share amongst everyone. The dogs had dried up watermelon that Molly had secretly stolen from her neighbour. She quickly climbed over the fence whilst they weren't looking and slipped the pieces into her pockets.

For entertainment, her birthday party consisted of playing knuckle bones with her family. There wasn't even a prize for the winner! No goody

bags, just sitting on the floor throwing sheep bones up in the air with the Labradors watching keenly. Every once in a while the dogs would spoil a game by catching one of the bones in its mouth and scurrying away into a corner of the kitchen to chew on it. When the game restarted with the retrieved bone, it was all gooey and sticky and smelt of rotten fish. Molly didn't particularly mind though. She didn't think birthdays were special anyway.

Chapter Three

The day after their birthday the fair came to town. Molly knew there was a fair because everywhere she turned she saw a large poster on a tree or a bus stop or a lamppost. She hopped on a bus which was free and it took her to the grand entrance to the fair. There was a long queue but Molly sneaked amongst the children who didn't

notice her as they were too excited to look.

However, one girl who was near the front did notice and said, "Don't push in!"

Another girl said, "Don't worry, you can queue with me." So Molly managed to get into the fair. She wandered around on her own for a while.

Eventually, Molly came across the bouncy castle. It was a big dome shaped inflatable

castle with see-through windows along the sides. In the front was a row of shoes and behind the row of shoes was a very fierce looking lady. She wore a blue jacket which had large orange buttons.

Molly asked the lady, "Please may I have a go on the castle?"

Although the lady looked fierce she wasn't fierce at all.

"Of course you may," she laughed.

Molly didn't wait to be told twice. She raced into the castle and before she could start jumping she bumped into a girl who looked familiar.

The girl looked back at Molly and said, "Ouch, look where you're going!"

"Sorry," said Molly. "I was just so excited to get on the castle."

"Excited?" said the girl. "Why would anyone be excited about this boring bouncy castle?"

To Molly the bouncy castle looked like an enormous enchanted castle that she had never seen before with an enormous jack-in-the-box on the roof.

Cici and Molly

Cici (the other girl) slipped into one of the grooves of the castle and fell over. Molly had never been on a bouncy castle before and she was

worried that Cici was hurt. "Are you alright?" asked Molly.

"Don't you know anything! This is a bouncy castle. You're meant to fall over!"

Molly felt hurt inside.

As soon as Cici realised what she had done she felt embarrassed. Cici

thought to herself that it was just a little girl; she didn't need to apologise.

Finally, Cici and Molly both hopped off.

Chapter Four

After the bouncy castle, Cici won four teddy bears – all the same kind - at the archery stall.

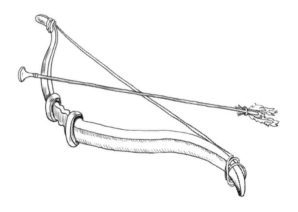

Everyone was jealous of her. A small girl approached Cici and begged, "Please can I have one of your teddy bears? You have four! I'll swap you for this bracelet."

"Ok, little girl, I'll swap with you...NOT!"

The little girl started to cry.

Cici had one last go at archery and this time won a black wig. She said to the man, "What a stupid prize." She felt like throwing it away as it smelt

awful. But then she had an idea. She would put the wig on and scare everybody in the Hall of Mirrors. Then she would have the whole place all to herself.

Cici approached the Hall of Mirrors triumphantly and walked inside.

At first it was dark and she bumped into something. It was cold and hard. She felt it and quickly realised it was just a mirror. She moved on. Next, the Hall became a

little lighter and she could see the next mirror; or was it a mirror? Cici wasn't sure exactly how she looked with a black wig on. When she poked the mirror she realised it wasn't made of glass. It was solid, like a person. Cici squinted to make out who it was. As her eyes adjusted to the poor light she realised it was the girl she met earlier at the bouncy castle. Cici stared at her for a minute thinking how alike they both looked. But then Cici thought to herself, I'll scare her anyway. Cici took off her wig and shouted,

"Raaaaaaaaaaaaaaaaaaaa!!"

Cici and Molly

But Molly was not scared at all. She was used to behaviour like that from her brothers.

"Why aren't you scared of me?" asked Cici.

"Well, I've got four brothers and they're always doing that," said Molly.

"Hi ya. My name is Molly, what's yours?"

"I'll give you a clue. It begins with C, and it ends in..."

"CICI!" exclaimed Molly.

Cici looked astounded. "How did you know that? I've never told you my name."

"Well my mum told me I had a twin sister," answered Molly.

"So? What's that got to do with me?" snorted Cici.

"I thought you looked familiar."

"So are you saying we're related?" asked Cici.

"Well I'm not exactly sure. But I

know how to find out. I've got this
clapping game we can do. It goes like
this."

Molly held her hands out in front of
Cici, palms up.

"Are you showing me how dirty your hands are?" asked Cici.

"No!" said Molly. "Just watch and listen. Ask questions at the end. What you do is clap my hands really hard.

Now ask me which one hurts the most. And then the hand of mine that

hurts the most you tickle each finger then ask me which tickled the most.

 Then what you do is the finger that was the most ticklish you put it out in front of me. Now you count how many lines you've got on that finger. Then you put your hands back out to the starting place and cross your hands over your shoulders.

Then you count the number of lines and that number of times you cross your hands underneath the other hand."

Cici was listening intently.

Molly continued, "And then you put your hands out still crossed and see if they knot together. If they knot then we are related. If they pull apart then we are not related."

Cici did as she was told. They put their hands out to see if they were related and...

Yes! They were related!

Chapter Five

Cici and Molly stared at each other. They couldn't believe they had stumbled upon a sister! They both burst out laughing and when they stopped laughing they hugged.

"Why don't you meet your Mum?" asked Molly.

"I've already got a Mum."

"I mean your real Mum."

"I don't want another one," Cici said.

"I think Mum would love to see you. There's no time for fussing, let's just do it," said Molly.

"Well ok, I'll do it. But before we go, let's have one last ride."

"Ok, let's go on the mat race. Just follow me," Molly said.

Suddenly, Cici's butler arrived. "Cici, it's time to go home now," he ordered.

"Ok, I'll meet you back at the car in five minutes."

Her butler returned to the car park.

"What are you doing?" asked Molly.

"You're meant to meet your
Mum!"

"Shhh. I have a plan," said Cici.

Cici started walking towards the car
where her butler was holding the door
open for her. But just before getting in

the back seat, Cici darted around the back of the car and disappeared out of sight.

"Where are you?" called Molly. Molly started looking in the direction of where Cici ran. The butler was looking around too. Because the car was so long he didn't know where to start!

He muttered to himself, "I wish I didn't work for this beastly girl!"

Cici, hiding behind a tree, overheard him and chuckled to herself, "I want to get rid of him anyway."

Molly went looking for Cici and soon found her.

"How did you know I was hiding here?" asked Cici.

"Because we're sisters. I know what you're thinking."

"What am I thinking right now then?"

"About meeting your Mum, I suppose."

Cici stared open-mouthed. She thought it was impossible to read

other people's minds.

"Come on. Let's go to my house," said Molly.

"Ok. I think I'm ready."

"But what about your butler?" asked Molly.

"Don't worry about him. He'll buy himself a nice cup of coffee and completely forget about me."

Molly led the way to her house.

Cici was scared about meeting her real Mum. She was worried about meeting her and not being welcomed.

Molly could see a worried expression on Cici's face.

"Don't worry, there's nothing to be

scared about. You'll like my dogs, they're very nice and they don't bite."

Cici thought this might be her only opportunity to meet her mum.

Molly opened the door. To Cici it sounded like a creak, rusty, like a crow without a beak. As they entered they saw Molly's brothers treating the dogs like they were toys. Molly ran up to her brothers and pushed them aside before they could do anything else. The boys looked up and down at Molly as if they had never seen her before.

"What did you do that for?" asked one of them.

"I don't want my guest to know how

horrible it is in this house sometimes."

"I'm Cici," Cici blurted out nervously, "I'm Molly's sister."

"Did you just say Cici?" Mum asked. She looked sternly at Molly. Her eyes looked like ice bolts were going to come out of them. "Answer me yes or no!"

"Yes," said Molly shakily.

"You are not to say that name ever again. Do you hear me?"

Mum couldn't bring herself to look at Cici again. She just turned around and fled to the kitchen.

Molly didn't dare speak a word. She held Cici's hand to comfort her and they both left the house.

Chapter Six

"So where are we going to meet?" asked Molly.

"We can't be friends at my house," said Cici.

"Why not?" replied Molly.

"I know what my Mum is like."

Just then an idea popped into Molly's mind. "I know exactly what we could

do. We can build a den and meet there."

"A den? How are we supposed to do that?"

"Well my father works as a builder and he taught me some building skills. First, we need to make a plan and a foundation. We need to find some good land, not too hilly, and not too rocky."

"I know the exact place," said Cici confidently. "In the woods, next to the river. No one would dream of us being there."

"Great," agreed Molly.

"So what are we waiting for? We need to get a pen and paper and draw the plan. But we also need planks and nails."

"I've got all those things at my house," said Cici. "Ok, please go and get them and meet me at the edge of the woods."

In the blink of an eye Cici ran to her house. In no time at all, Cici was back

to the woods with all the things they needed.

They found a nice secluded spot amongst some trees where their secret den would be built.

"I brought a rubber in case we make some mistakes. Let's just draw the plan. First, we need to dig the

Cici and Molly

foundation. Draw that on the plan and I'll start digging. Next, we need to start putting the wood on the foundation."

"Wait, you're going too fast," said Cici.

"Why don't we just draw the plan first then make the building?"

"Ok. So you've done the foundation. Now you need to draw the wood."

"Are we going to put the wood horizontally or vertically?" questioned Cici.

"Well I guess it will be easier to do it vertically so you can dig the wood in

more easily. Let's start," said Molly.

"Start drawing?" Cici asked.

"Just draw how you think it should look."

"Done!" said Cici after a few minutes went by.

"I'll take a look at it. Great. Perfect. Now first what we have to do is measure how long the walls should be."

Cici said, "I think about two meters

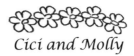

Cici and Molly

will be best."

Suddenly, the girls heard a sound.
"What was that?" Cici exclaimed.

Kasia Brown

Molly looked in the distance.

"Oh my gosh, it's my brothers. We can't let them find the den!" said Molly. "Otherwise they'll take it over and never let us come into it. And we won't have a secret place to meet."

Cici got upset and started crying.

"Don't worry, Cici. I have a plan," said Molly. "Here is a cardboard tube. If you speak into it you sound like a robot. When they come near us they will probably ask us what we are doing. All you have to say is we are making a robot that destroys all boys. And if they ask to prove it, then you say: 'Bring out the robot.'

Then I will shout through the tube 'destroy all boys, destroy all boys, destroy all boys.'"

As the boys approached, Cici did as she was told and Molly sounded like a very convincing robot.

Molly's brothers were extremely frightened and they ran away home.

"Pheww. That was close," said Cici.

Molly looked up at the sky. "It's getting dark. My mum will be worried."

Cici looked sad and didn't want to go home and didn't want to leave the den unfinished.

"We'll meet up again next Saturday,"

reassured Molly.

They carefully hid their materials under some branches and leaves.

"Don't forget to take the plan," said Cici.

Molly carefully rolled the plan up and put it safely in her pocket like it was a solid bar of gold. They both returned to their own separate homes.

Until the following Saturday they thought of nothing but the den. Would it be discovered?

All week at school Cici acted quite strangely because she could think of nothing else but the den. She was obsessed about it. Every day as soon

as she woke up she studied her
calendar. She looked at her watch
during class and almost got scolded
for fiddling with it during maths.

Cici was also thinking about the
awful time she had with her mum
when she got rejected from the home

where she was born before she was adopted out. Cici thought Molly was the most special person she had ever met and she couldn't wait to see her again on Saturday. She thought about the den and how Molly would be the closest family member she'd ever had.

During Molly's week she was thinking exactly the same thoughts as Cici.

She was determined to get back to

the forest quickly but it was still five days away. It felt like a year! As she treasured her secret plan she always took a few moments to look at it. She thought about her best friend Cici. Her parents even said Molly was talking in her sleep about a best friend but Molly didn't reveal that it was Cici.

It was Thursday - just two days to go – and Molly was out walking the dogs on the street. She didn't know her brothers had snuck in to her room and were looking around, trying to find something in her room.

"What's under the bed?" one of them said and started to lift up the corner of

Kasia Brown

her mattress.

"I don't know, it might be a great place to hide a..."

"What are you doing?" Molly screeched. She got back just in the nick of time!

"Nothing," her brothers mumbled.

"Get out," she said and pointed to the door. She really, really didn't want them to keep looking around.

They dropped the mattress and filed out of her room.

"Phew, that was close," she thought. They could have spoilt everything!

Molly thought when she was a bit younger that since she belonged to a

Cici and Molly

poor family, she wouldn't have any friends. But when she met Cici she thought what a good friend she was. Their den was the only place they could meet up since her mum didn't want to hear about Cici. If anyone found their den they would never be able to see each other again.

Chapter Seven

The following Saturday, as arranged, they met back at the den.

The den walls were built and it was now time for the exciting part - building the roof.

"Cici, you do one side and I'll do the other," shouted Molly as if she was a teacher.

When the girls had finished they stepped back to admire their work.

Kasia Brown

And last, but not least, they put two
stools inside. After that they went
inside. Molly looked at it as she said,

Cici and Molly

"There's something missing."

Cici looked disappointed because she worked hard on this den with Molly but now she had to keep building. She was almost out of breath.

Molly said, "We need a trap door, Cici."

"What do we need a trap door for?" exclaimed Cici.

"If we don't have a secret way in and out, we might get trapped inside! You never know when we might need to use it," Molly said.

"Great idea!" Cici said. "I would feel safer too if we had one."

63

But before Cici could utter another word, Molly was already a quarter of the way through building it.

"How could you start it without me?"

But Molly was struggling.

"Why don't I help you," said Cici in a helpful voice. She grabbed the spade. But she could not dig into the ground because it was

so hard from a lack of rain.

Just then, an idea popped into Molly's head. "Why don't we get one of my dogs to dig?" She whipped out a whistle from her pocket and blew into it.

In a second, Cici could see four yellow specks in the distance. As she looked closer, she could see they were Molly's dogs.

Cici asked, "How are we going to get them to dig?"

"We will hide a bone in a heap of soil

Kasia Brown

for each dog and then the dog who can dig the deepest can be the trap door digger. But we also need to set a booby trap in case any unwanted people approach. We have to dig a really deep hole and put leaves and twigs on the top especially thorns and stinging nettles."

"Ok but we'll probably need the rest of the dogs to dig the booby trap." In two hours, they had finished both.

"I love it!" Cici stated as she looked over their new additions. "Me too! A trap door and a booby trap, so we are completely safe inside now."

Chapter Eight

The girls had been very busy and they were tired. But they admired their den.

Cici said to Molly, "I feel tired. Let's have a short ten minute nap."

"Good idea," said Molly.

So they dropped down into their cosy beds and snuggled down like

new-born chicks.

The girls had snuck some hay from the neighbour's field. They made two piles next to each other near the trap door.

Ten minutes later, they hadn't woken up. They were still asleep!

They slept through the whole night without even knowing it!

Cici and Molly

At dawn they woke up. They could hear faint cries, people calling in the distance.

What was going on?

As they appeared with their small titchy eyes out of the window they could see who was coming: it was everyone they knew! There were Molly's and Cici's mums, Molly's brothers, her dogs and her dad. Cici's butler, cleaner, entertainer, tennis coach, swimming tutor, maid, nanny and servants and last and least she thought she saw her maths teacher (whom she hated the most).

They stared at the whole party. Was their secret den going to be discovered? Would they destroy the den and prohibit Cici and Molly meeting and being friends? They approached the den but didn't fall into

the booby trap because Cici's maths teacher spotted it somehow.

The search party was almost upon them! Then Molly had an idea. She picked up the last bone they'd used to make the dogs dig the trap door. Molly

threw the bone over the search party and into the river. The dogs saw the bone

and dove after it. Everyone wondered what the dogs had smelt and went running away from the secret den and towards the river.

Eventually, they got the dogs out of the river but they were all wet so the dogs gave up and headed home.

"Now!" whispered Molly to Cici.

And as quick as a flash they both escaped through the trap door of the S.D.O.C.M. (Secret Den of Cici and Molly). That's what they called it for short.

They ran and ran. Their feet were

eating up the grass. They ran and ran until they were breathless. By the time they

got to their houses they were huffing and puffing as if they had just run a marathon.

Cici opened the door to her bedroom and flopped down on her bed. Just then, a whole crowd of people burst into the room relieved with joy that she had returned.

Her mother asked," Where have you been young lady?"

The butler demanded, "Where were you?"

Cici didn't know what to say. These people were all out looking for her and Molly?

The maths teacher said, "Cici, we

were so worried."

"We've spent hours searching," the housekeeper declared.

Cici felt sheepish but happy they had missed her.

"Sorry," Cici grinned. "I was in the library and it was closing time but I didn't want to go because I was in the middle of a book so they locked it up with me inside. So I had to sleep there."

Of course you all know (or whoever is reading this book) that Cici made up all the library stuff but she could not tell anyone about Molly and Cici's den or their friendship would be

destroyed!

Molly ran home and had to be very quiet sneaking in her back door. The family and dogs were heading in the front door at almost the same time!

"Oh no," Molly said and held her breath. She had to get up the stairs before the door opened and they burst in before she got to bed.

She pushed the door open and bolted up the stairs. She had just slipped into bed when the dogs burst through the front door and up the stairs to her room.

"What's going on?" Her brothers and mum asked.

"I just woke up, I don't know." Molly whispered, pretending she was sleepy. "What are you doing?"

Her brothers shrugged and went to their room. Her mum and dad looked at each other and didn't know what to say besides, "Good morning."

Molly was keeping the secret where she was and nobody knew any

Cici and Molly

different!

Cici and Molly met every day in their secret den. Not just as sisters but best friends for, well, forever.

Kasia Brown

Cici and Molly's Secret Milkshake

Ingredients:

Lemonade

Ice Cream

Grenadine

Tall glasses

Straws

1. Get the glass and scoop in some ice cream of your choice.
2. Pour some lemonade into the glass. It is perfectly fine if you see lots of foam on top.
3. Pour in a few drops of grenadine.
4. Pop in a straw.
5. Enjoy on a nice sunny day!

Cici and Molly

Printed in Great Britain
by Amazon.co.uk, Ltd.,
Marston Gate.